The mysteries of Tyson Wolf:

Wolf's Fury

AF541013

Harshit Bhasin

Invincible Publishers

First published in India in 2018

©2018 Harshit Bhasin, All Rights Reserved

ISBN: 978-93-87328-94-5

No part of this publication may be reproduced or stored in a retrieval system, or transmitted in any form or by any means, electronic, mechanical, photocopying, recording or otherwise, without the prior permission of the publishers.

Invincible Publishers

G-120, Sushant Lok III, Sector 57, Gurgaon-122002

Registered Address: Opposite Kasturba Ashram,
Radaur, Haryana - 135133

Cover Design by Ashish Samant

Printed at Thomson Press (India) LTD

To Professor Ramon O. Torres-Isea of the University of Michigan, Ann Arbor, USA for his never ending wisdom and inspiration.

ACKNOWLEDGEMENT

This book has been possible by the blessings of God and the best wishes of my family and friends.

A special thanks to my parents, school and my teachers for their unending support and enthusiasm. Also, a vote of gratitude goes to my close friends Tanish Baweja, Praneet Sawhney, Shaurya Jain and Samridhi Ghai for their support, inspiration and presence.

Thank you everyone for being there for me and in helping me get this book to completion.

PREFACE

The starry sky gives way to the sun, the night recedes its clutches from the world and the day takes its place, the light purges the dark, until the cycle is repeated.

This is the way of life, various phases of light and dark, day and night, but such is not the situation for all. There are some who are forever lost in the dark, while for some the cycle breaks and they enter the peaceful wings of death.

That night, the ravens crooned as if relaying a message from death, the sky was cloudy and a light drizzle was falling as if even the heavens were crying for the recent loss of life.

But when has that ever stopped anyone? After all, it is the fate of mankind to always go on. In this cruel world that never sleeps and sends cruel reminders to people to stay on their guard, a life that saved many is destroyed forever, thrown into the darkness, destined to be the spark of light that shall forever remain in the dark, the speck of hope that, as if punished, is kept alive with that feeling of despair, never allowed to go out, never allowed to give up.

CHAPTER 1

This was supposed to be the last night in the case of a series of murders that had the whole town gripped in fear of death. Lead forensic investigator, Tyson Wolf, had volunteered to become the bait for the case, after all, it was his duty to save the town (He liked to fool himself by thinking that he was overly important for the city's safety). He felt eerily lonely in his expedition, with a sinking feeling in his heart that something was about to go wrong and it would weigh upon his conscience in a way that he would never be able to forgive or forget. But he ignored it, after all, what could go wrong, it was horribly simple, even though he did not have the support of the minimum required personnel or even the clearance to undergo this operation. The truth was that his entire department might have helped him win his foolishness if they had known, but he was doing it without their knowledge because then he would not have been able to fulfill his idiotic desire to become a lead investigating officer. He was tired of sitting in labs with nothing to challenge his impulsive nature. He wanted to be out in the field and put his talent to some use. He wouldn't have been in this position, had he not refused to bribe the instructor who had then changed his test result and failed him. The truth was that he was solving this case without the knowledge of the department, as it was a dangerous yet important business and they were hesitant to put the lives of anyone in their department in danger. Only a few of his fellow officers and friends knew about it. They were hiding near the alley to stop the killer if he attacked him; after all, that was the plan.

He was doing all this for two motives: to prove himself, to win the respect that he had lost after being declared unworthy of becoming an investigating officer, and to make the town safe, not for everyone, that would have been a selfless motive and despite what he liked to show, he wasn't a selfless person. He just wanted to make the town safer for his brother-Anthony, for he was all that mattered to him in his life.

He continued to walk towards his destination, trying his best to walk casually, this was the most significant aspect of their plan. The killer could not know that he was under supervision, that this was the last time he would be attempting a murder.

The basic plan was for him to go into the alley acting as if he was searching for something.

The air had a chill of death in it. It reeked of death and decay as if trying to warn him. People were hurrying back home for they were sick with fear but not the man in the khaki coat. He couldn't turn back; the situation wouldn't allow it. His face was well-known and at the moment, it was covered with determination, pride, and fearlessness (He was a good actor, the truth was that he was shaking with fear). To cover this visage, he wore a matching hat.

The wind was howling in his ears. He was least bothered as he had been to a lot of cold places; one of them being his own lab. His only cause of worry was his new coat. Though he wasn't materialistic, he didn't want it to get ruined. This coat was a gift from his brother Anthony. So, he wished that the alley floor wouldn't destroy it, after all, it wouldn't be just if the khaki color was damaged.

He reached the alley. It was dark and damp. Well... there goes his hope for his coat. The alley was filled with places where sly cats could easily hide. He had his eyes for only one, one that would fulfil his dream: to utilize the much feared wolf's fury. It was his secret ability, the way he could channel his anger in a structured way. This led to his wrath being feared for it never ends well for those on whom it's focused on, whether he knows them or not. Known or unknown they were destroyed.

When he was about twenty steps in the alley, he felt a lurking figure move behind a garbage can. It moved from one corner to another with surprising agility. This was the first time our heroin distress had witnessed such speed and agility. He felt a chill run down his spine. The temperature went down another degree and all determination vanished from his face; it was now painted with fear. He was vulnerable now. Fear makes a man cautious, and in this town, cautiousness led to death. This was exactly what the cat wanted.

Everyone around could feel this sudden change. But no one knew whether it was true or an imitation.

Tyson turned around, his face betraying his attempts to remain calm. His survival instinct were finally weakening his resolve. The sly cat could smell his fear, it grew more confident, preying upon it to grow more powerful, more arrogant, and more foolish.

This was going very well and unless some momentous error took place, this mission would be successful.

He knew very well that the reason of death in all cases a sudden shock to the heart due to a needle coated green with inland taipan venom. To any forensic expert worth his salt this was a big red flag but he was wearing a vest that would protect him from needles and his friends were there to help if he was attacked. His survival instinct was telling him to turn back, he suppressed it. This was becoming more difficult to control. He just hoped that it wouldn't get any worse.

"Leave it to the human nature to compromise a mission," he thought.

"Who is it?" he shouted in a trembling voice, "come out, I won't hurt you."

"Yeah, right. Of course, I said that" he thought.

He cautiously moved towards the can, taking slow steps doing his best to hide his almost-cheerful-yet-scared demeanor. Suddenly, a hand with blazing speed and agility came and struck a needle in his protected chest.

He was constantly assured that the vest would also absorb the shock that he would no doubt face, well apparently that was all for show. That hurt!

The needle didn't touch his flesh but he let gravity take its toll and fell as if he were dead. He used his years of meditation training and calmed his breath, stilled his twitching muscles, performing to his best abilities the role of a dead body.

Then the figure came with a knife in his hand. Its face was swollen red covered with a mask which gave it the look of a mummy. He had an aura of death around him. It smelt of the dead. The ghastly face scared people out of their wits, a cruel sneer was painted on the mask and its eyes seemed to glint in the dark. He wore a black overcoat and tight pants. He was bald and his face resembled the cruel pharaoh Khufu. He was quite tall, in fact, he was one of the tallest men, Tyson had ever seen in his entire life. Then he noticed his sandals.

"Curious", he thought "why would he wear these? They would obviously hinder his balance and therefore hinder his kills. He should prefer bare feet or the like."

He advanced closer and stopped as if looking at Tyson's very soul, analyzing him as if he were a problem to be solved and then took a step back as if noticing that something was amiss.

"Does he know something," thought Tyson, dumbstruck.

The figure continued to retreat as if he knew better than to stay here any longer. He looked flustered.

Suddenly, he was shot in the leg and his progress stopped. The man twitched violently and his mask fell off. He quickly removed his necklace and tried to take the cyanide pill that was inside. But the doctor, who was hiding with Tyson's other friends, ran and quickly knocked the pill out of his hand. He then proceeded to punch the already shot man in the face and stepped back to observe his handiwork. The person in question was now clutching his foot. He was also smiling. This was strange; usually, a man who had just been caught on the crime scene looks like a little boy caught with his hand in the cookie jar. This man was different, he looked like a little kid who had just found a candy store.

He was a man with cat-like orange eyes, though it was quite possible that he was wearing contact lenses. He had scars covering his face yet looked what many would call ruggedly handsome. His most notable feature, however, was a tattoo. It looked like a hieroglyphic but was unrecognizable due to the dark.

Then all of Tyson's allies walked out of their respective outposts. Tyson's best friend, Detective Trevor Chase, walked towards the injured man and read him his rights. With the arrest complete they swarmed around Wolf.

Hugs were bestowed upon our hero and it took all of his effort to make sure that he did not yell at them.

"He is either senile or very, very brave," officer Sterling said, "but well done, Wolf!"

Wolf's chest swelled with pride. After all, it wasn't everyday that you make an arrest that you were not even supposed to make, especially in a case as high profile as this.

The backup unit and the ECU arrived minutes later and the man was packed into a police van. He was composed and was not struggling as if he knew that it was pointless and he could not escape. This was beyond comprehension. Even though it was his first time in the field, he knew that such behavior was only showcased when the person had a plan, one they couldn't even think about at the moment.

The man was loaded onto a van and was shipped off to the station. As Tyson watched the blue van move out of the street with its red sirens buzzing he breathed a sigh of relief. He had just realized how lucky he was that he was safe and unharmed after such an attack. He murmured a silent thanks to the almighty God because of whom he was alive. He knew that he would probably face the wrath of the superintendent, but he would take pleasure init. He started walking away from the place, determined never to take such a risk again without a strong reason. Which meant that anyone who had a chance to hurt his brother made that list. He was one impulsive and emotional man.

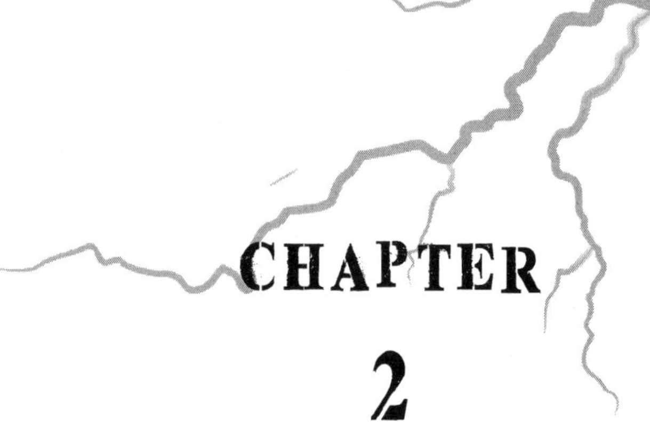

CHAPTER 2

After a long night at the police station, the man hailed as a hero, Tyson Wolf finally returned home.

He had a long day filling paperwork at the police station. Now he realized why policemen were always grumpy, after all, who wouldn't be when you catch a criminal, take a low life off the streets, and what do you get? A day off the field and on the desk doing paperwork! Who cares about the paperwork when you can hire someone to do it. Someone whose job description was solely to do paperwork. He had just taken down a criminal who was responsible for multiple murders, some even suspected that he was the gang leader, yet instead of building off of the lead he had gotten them, they were all taking a break.

His house was in the same state he had left it in the morning two days ago. Quite right, he had been out for two days in a row, completing the formalities.

His peach colored couch stared at him enticingly, as if luring him towards it but he had to resist it. He hadn't seen his brother in two days and now was the time to do it.

He walked around the house looking for his younger brother. He first went to the only room in the house, the one that belonged to his brother. It was in a state of disarray that shouted out to anyone who knew the two brothers even marginally that it belonged to Anthony. He was a kid who preferred chaos, unlike his brother who prefers order with certain aspects of chaos mixed with it. This room also had a sentimental value attached. It looked frighteningly similar to the way it had looked back when their father had been alive.

John Wolf had been a man of his word; a policeman who aspired to clear the streets of every single low life in the city. At least that was what his two sons had been told. He had vanished in thin air when Tyson was fourteen. His mother had died of heartbreak and Tyson was left with his family's responsibility. The only good thing was that they had the house and their father's pension, for he was presumed dead. The day after this presumption was made, Tyson decided to enrol for the academy. After the hurtful rejection, he had lost everything. Thank god for one of his dad's old friends that he was able to enroll in a college and get a job as a forensic expert. Not his dream job, but really close to it.

There was an old cupboard in the corner of the room. It was made of dark oak and had a regal finish. A similar bed adorned the center of the room. It had a royal blue cover on top of it. Spread across the room were hundreds of books and pictures. Except all this, the room was pretty bare. Also, Anthony was not there, so he went out of the room.

His next stop was the kitchen. It was styled in the similar modest fashion as the rest of the house. The only factor that seemed to lighten the room was the sight of his brother sitting on the wooden stool.

He was wearing a dark blue shirt and shorts. He was a nice, tall kid who looked like a mini version of Tyson except that he had blue eyes. The minute he saw Tyson he grinned impishly, it seemed to split his face into two.

Tyson pulled another stool and sat facing him.

"Listen to me kiddo, this is very important," Tyson began, "You know what happened in that alley two nights ago?"

"Hmm... yeah," Anthony said, looking confused.

"So, now they are going to re-evaluate my final test at the academy," continued a very exited Tyson.

"Why?"

"Well... you see, the chief asked them to do it in light of recent events."

"And you just believed that?"

"Anthony, I know you have always been a bit skeptical of the department since that day..."

"Since the day you...you, my brother, not me was cheated out of your hard earned right."

"Well, when you put it like that... but we can correct it now."

"No, we cannot. We are still paying for what they did that day. You may not believe it but I know that this will not end well for any of us."

With this decisive line, he stood up and walked out. A crestfallen Tyson stared after his brother. OH! How he hated when things like this happened. He had spent his entire life trying to take care of Anthony and being close to his father's memory, and now that he was getting a chance to do something he wanted, this was how he was to face it.

He suddenly realized that his brother had gone out of the house in a fit of anger, this was something he hadn't done since he was thirteen. He was usually very understanding. The fact that the situation was playing out like this left a pit in his stomach.

CHAPTER 3

It was a new moon night. The whole town was under a power cut. A dry wind was blowing across the town and it looked like a violent storm was about to strike. As such, Anthony Wolf, the brother of a forensic expert and future detective Tyson Wolf, walked through a dark alley where his brother had arrested the culprit in a series of gruesome murders. He was a man of lean build at the age of nineteen and played soccer at his university. He ran a hand through his messy hair, a habit he shared with his brother.

He felt guilty that he had shouted at his brother in such a manner. This was usually not like him but he, he had just lost control when he heard that they were going to have his brother go through it all again. His brother, despite his good intentions and talents, was naïve. He was loyal to anyone who showed even a speck of loyalty and herein lied his fault. This was a cruel world and people loved to take advantage of those who tried to help them. His brother was good-natured; he might seem like a prankster who didn't care for anyone but himself and his brother but that was not the case, it had been before their father had vanished but since that day, his idiot of a brother had started to care.

He had meant this as a field trip to feel pleasure in what his brother had done. It was also meant to give him some idea as to what his brother was going to be doing from now on. He would just have to deal with it. The truth was, he didn't want to lose his brother the way he had lost his father. Tyson thought that he didn't remember their father, but he did, and it hurt him every single moment of his life.

Looking at the set up around him, his chest swelled with pride. He started thinking of how he would blabber about this to his friends, how he would try to make them jealous of it. If he could not stop his brother he would at least take advantage of him gallivanting around the city with a badge.

He stopped to look at the point where his brother had played dead in front of the man he had arrested. Oh, what a spot it was with the muddy ground and the stench of death. It was perfect for the purpose they used it.

He continued to go around looking and admiring the spot, filing stuff away for later reference. He was feeling uneasy; the temperature was going down by the second.

Anthony felt a shadowy figure lurking behind him. He turned around to see a humanoid figure creep behind a garbage can like a swift cat. It was not a coincidence that this was happening in the same way his brother had described.

Worried, he tiptoed towards the can. As soon as he looked behind the can a small needle pierced his chest and he died instantly.

From behind the can, a man with a cloak crept out from behind it. His face was covered, but he had a regal aura. His body was painfully upright and he walked with a malicious intent.

He surveyed the body with a sense of odd satisfaction that he had never felt before. (The body was laying peacefully. But the cruel murderer just wouldn't leave the body in a proper manner, it lessened the sense of content.)

He took a knife and carved out all the vitals except the heart. He knew that the reason he had to do this was personal and that this might get him in trouble. But he did not care. After all, everything is fair in love and war and the little Wolf had started a war that would break him.

CHAPTER 4

Before entering the police station, Tyson tried calling his brother's cell phone. The call was directed to voicemail. He feared that something bad might have happened as he had not returned home since the other night. Then entered Captain James as the police people called him. He was wearing a blue shirt and a three-piece suit over it. His blonde hair was plastered to his face, he was lean with bulging muscles. He was wearing shoes that looked like they had just been washed, although there were some red stains on the sole. Tyson felt suspicious but then let it go thinking that the captain might be returning from a crime scene. This was unlikely, for if he were coming from a crime scene and had to wash his shoes he would have done it with bleach to completely remove the stains The captain smiled and hugged Tyson. He whispered his news in a way that only the two of them could hear it. Tyson jumped with happiness. This was his first real case which was assigned to him by the department. He knew nothing about the case except that the body had been dealt with extreme cruelty. There were several cuts on the body, this murder was just like the one that he had just solved.

Upon reaching the scene, he saw that people were crowded along the police line. Police were trying their best to make sure that no one came inside the bright yellow ribbon. All his colleagues were sweating and trying to persuade Tyson to give this case up.

Something was definitely wrong. This was not supposed to happen!

But he was adamant and pushed several of his friends out of the way.

"Wolf, I think you might wanna let this case go after all you have just accomplished," Chase said in a trembling voice.

"Chase, if you don't leave this instant, I will not be at fault for what happens next."

Fighting with half the department is not easy. It should not have been required at all! After all, what had happened that they were all acting like this?

Chucking a couple of choice words at others, he pushed up the police tape. With his back towards the body, he made a joke about them behaving as if it was Anthony who had died.

He turned around with his gloves in hand and saw something that took the life out of him. There, lying on cardboard boxes, was his life, his family, his brother, Anthony. His hair stuck to his forehead, matted with dry blood. The bright blue eyes had lost all of their spark.

He couldn't handle it. He broke down, falling down on the dirty alley floor, his heart breaking into a million pieces. He screamed till his throat burnt raw. How could this happen? It was supposed to be over. He had already caught the murderer; the gang was supposed to be over, gone, destroyed.

Feeling the wetness of blood on his head, he finally stood up- there was still work to be done.

A war had begun, one that had already destroyed him, but who was he, if not a Wolf? They may have won the battle, now they will be destroyed.

He looked around for clues, there wasn't much there. His only leads were a couple of footprints.

This was weird. Usually, this did not happen. No killer was kind enough to leave footprints, and a killer who was any good would never leave such evidence. It was as if they were calling for him, taunting him, challenging him.

Oh well, turns out the war is two sided.

The new forensics expert called for Tyson. Reaching there, he was told that his brother was missing his kidneys, lungs, and brain; but he already knew that. He had checked a lot of victims of this gang and the common trait in these murders was that the body always missed some important parts.

It was as if they were trying to do the police a favor by finishing half of the autopsy so they wouldn't have to do so much work. This had been a joke in the lab. They'd often said that they were forensic experts in training who were just practicing.

Not for the life of them, had they expected that this would happen to Tyson's brother but Tyson was sure that it was revenge that had taken his life.

Now it was this revenge that would lead him to the gang. This was the last straw to unleash the ultimate fury of all, Wolf's fury- he had been famous for this back at the academy. This was the true form of his impulsive nature.

All he needed to do for now was to make a statement in the press telling the public to stay away from such alleys and other places like this, especially if they were empty, and to tell those people who had killed his brother that now they were going to be victims of his fury and that he would catch each and every one of them.

Being this furious also brought out his most hidden trait: cunning. The first part of the statement would be made immediately but the second, it would not be spoken. Oh no, it would be delivered. After all, actions speak louder than words.

There was another, deeper, reason for hiding his anger in a box for some time. Until he had a lead that led him straight to the gang or one of its main members, he couldn't afford to be blind to evidence.

So, for now, he would just write a letter to his seniors telling them that he seeked permission to conduct a hard-core interrogation with the killer he had caught.

CHAPTER 5

The latest development in the case was that Captain James had denied his request for torture. The captain thought that this would be a violation of human rights.

Who cared for human rights? Certainly not the one he was planning to violate it on. It would be stupid since the guy would be sentenced to death anyways. Why not just make his death a little useful.

Another thing that irked him to no end was that he was quoting the Geneva Convention when it didn't even apply in this case! He felt it was very stupid.

Well, according to him all this is stupid beyond thought. Unfortunately, the Captain is the captain and he couldn't really say anything if he didn't want to be fired.

Sam, a tech head and one of his fellows, called him. He is a nice and tall guy with a mischievous glint in his blue eyes.

"Hey Wolf, wassup?" he began in his forever merry tone.

"Buzz off, Sam! Go tinker with some computers or something, I'm not in the mood for your stupid jokes."

"Well, someone's in a mood. I came here to tell you that I can help you. We can always see what happens in the city. But as you so eloquently put it, I will just..."

Saying this, he started to walk out. Thinking about what he said a figurative light lit up above Tyson's head- cameras! This was the sign he had been searching for. The stress was getting to him, how could he ignore something so obvious.

“Hey Sam,”, Tyson called,” I’m sorry. Can you help me?”

“Course, what do you need?”

“Sam, I want you to scout for all cameras in a five-mile radius around the alley. Get me anything you can. I know that in the past this trick has failed us but now I have a feeling that it will work.”

“Ooh, five miles? On it boss, you’ll have a preliminary response by tomorrow.”

“Thanks, Sam, I knew I could trust you.”

Saying this, Tyson walked out of the station. Standing on the edge of the stairs, he looked at the town he loved. The sound of traffic, its crowded nature. Looking at all the people he wondered only one thing- How in the world was he going to find a person he knew nothing about in this town.

CHAPTER 6

On the other hand, the individual in question was building his gang once again as he knew that he had to do something or else they would soon be behind bars. He was not a newbie in the business. He had been doing this for a long time. The only reason he had survived this long was that he carefully planned everything he did. He knew that despite the arrest of one of their members, they were not in danger. But that was all in the past. What a cruel world it was, the man who taught the entire gang how to sneak, scout, and more importantly to kill without leaving a single clue had left a bloody footprint. Who even does that anymore? Footprints were over-rated. Well, now nothing could be done. He had left one and now he had to deal with it, now he had a war to prepare for. He had to fight this war from out in the shadows.

A sharp knock on the door brought him out of his stupor. He looked about the room in wonder as if thinking about how he had gotten there.

“Come in,” he said in a regal yet cold voice.

With that sharp command, in walked the cavalry, the entire gang. The idiots in the administration think that they were a bunch of wannabees, well, this will teach them.

In the dungeon filled with hundreds of people dressed in regal battle armor. The armors were green with highlights of blue and black. All of them bowed.

The scene seemed oddly fitting in the room. The corners were lit with torches. The flames seemed to dance with a strange grace as if already enjoying the battle that was about to ensue.

“Welcome friends! We meet at a new crossroad. The stupid administration has caught one of our members," he started with a tone that was warm, yet cold.

At this, there was a sharp intake of breath from the crowd. The entire army stood up in sync and the room was filled with the sounds of a gong. This was the sound of all of them banging their arms on their breastplates.

"They made their move and I made mine. I have killed that imbecile's brother," he continued.

At this, everyone banged the feet on the ground, at a time difference of two seconds with a precision that would have made any military man proud.

"It is now a war. The question isthatdo we let them win or do we destroy them? Remember your oath brothers!"

All of them walked towards the big throne that the orator was sitting on. They removed their masks and put them on the floor while kneeling. A sign of complete submission. This was all the proof needed that one side of the army was armed and ready to move.

"Leave now brothers and gather our allies. This is our chance to complete the mission that we swore to fulfill."

They filed out and were ready to take action. Their calm and calculated strides were marked with a strange confidence and determination. A casual bystander looking at them would have wished that he was not the one they were targeting.

After their exit, the general was left alone with his plans. He removed his mask and sighed. He was getting too old. He would win this war and oh boy! It was going to be a massacre.

He stood up and walked towards the wall. Tapping two of the stones revealed a bulletin board. The board had the map of the entire town. There were also pictures of deserted yet frequented alleys of the city. These pictures were just of the high-profile ones. His attention was focused on one thing and one thing alone- picture of a young man. The man had no idea of the war he had just started. This was the man who will be decorated for taking action, but people will ignore the fact that he brought on the war.

Tyson Wolf was going to regret his entire existence. He touched the map of the city, it became enlarged. Contrary to popular belief the man didn't live in the dark ages. He quite liked his board. The map of the city showed all cameras of the city. He wanted a war so he needed to make sure that he did it correctly. Till now they always gave their customary signal to the cameras as a way of mocking before vanishing into the night. From now on, the killings would give a message, one that will be left for all to see.

The town called them the 'Mummifyrs'. What a stupid name! They had no idea who they were dealing with. The Order of the Double Falcon had arrived. Till now they had been content with living in the shadows but now they had a goal.

Very few people knew that the pharaoh had a motive, a vision which they were seeking to fulfill.

CHAPTER 7

Tyson had taken one of Anthony's shirts to wear while he met the expert who would help him in the war. The department thought this was just another case and he was quite happy with letting them believe just that.

In the past, he had often used the help of one of the more open-minded gangs in the city. These gangs just cared about themselves and everyone loved Anthony, even these crooks. So his brother would contact them whenever Tyson had a suspicion but wondered if it was true (After all, he didn't build his entire reputation as a

Forensics Expert who made dead bodies speak with just skill).

He was sure that if he used his brother's cell and looked a bit like him, that man would come out to meet him. He would just have to convince him that he meant no harm and just needed help in avenging Anthony. He knew for a fact that this man loved his brother like his own brother. These people are dangerous in normal situations and they are downright deadly if one of them is hurt.

The hard part was getting in contact with these people. Anthony was a tech genius. He had developed a new encryption system for phones and it was active on his phone. Getting something out of it was like fishing for sharks in a fish tank.

Tyson knew that the number was saved with a passcode and he did not know the name with which he had stored the number. He unlocked the phone and a strange music started to play, it was different each time someone unlocked his brother's phone; another one of his brother's programs, he had been told. Tyson stared at the blue screen for a moment for the phone to truly activate. This was a function to make sure that it was someone regular and not someone who wanted to steal information. His brother had been downright paranoid, but considering the things that Tyson made him do, it was justified. After activation, he saw the usual message: 'Hello Wolf!'. The screen was now that of any usual phone. Opening the contacts, he set about the task of checking all the contacts.

In his search, he found Marry, Lolita, Amy, etc. A normal brother would maybe look for a possible girlfriend but he knew that these were all code names. After all, his brother had listed his number as 'The Frilly Howler'.

This was normal but none of them had a passcode. he would've had Sam do it but he knew that if anyone, whose fingerprints are not registered in the system, touches the phone they get a shock and the phone goes in sleep mode.

This was a pretty good addition, but useless in choice situations. He found a name with red highlight. This contact was named 'Danger' and had a passcode on it.

Tyson knew this was the person he was looking for, after all, there was no one who scared his brother. If he is impulsive, Anthony was impulsiveness personified.

Tyson dialed the number and asked the person on the other side to meet him. His accent was familiar but be couldn't judge anything from it. This could mean only two things- that he was too stressed or that he relied on Anthony too much to get things done. Neither made him feel better.

The address he got was that of an alley which was usually deserted and dark. This was a bright red flag, but after the murders in other alleys, a lot of street lamps had been installed. He called the department to give him a bug sweeper along with the shoe case in case someone was watching him.

He left for the alley and felt a negative presence around him but ignored it as he couldn't do anything about it. The alley was brightly lit, he was afraid that his new friend wouldn't come to such brightly lit place. The alley was surrounded with houses and there were no garbage cans so he was free of the fear of death. The third house on the right had decorations and it looked different from all the other houses. The door was slightly open. He was afraid in case someone shot him from there. He ignored this feeling as he was doing this for the law, order, and his brother.

Then there was a loud noise and the nearest street light exploded then all lights started exploding one after other.

Then the door of the second house on his left opened. Similarly, all the other doors opened and someone ran towards me from behind. What shocked him was the sheer speed of the attack. It was so quick that before he could react, he was blindfolded.

Someone walked out from the door to his right. He then heard the same voice he had heard on the phone but it was a bit heavier and louder.

"Who are you? I was supposed to meet Anthony, not someone who would nab us. So, tell me who are you?" the voice asked.

"I am Tyson Wolf, Anthony's brother. I am here to ask for your help regarding his murder. You must have heard of the murderers who attack people in the alleys and then carve out their vital organs. I had recently arrested one of their gang members and then they attacked Anthony. My actions caused his death."

Growls could be heard from all around him. Now he was really scared. Sudden realisation of the fact that unless he started talking he would find a bullet embedded in his head hit him.

"The gang has now initiated a war and I intend to win it; but I can't do it alone, I need your help. Help me avenge my brother, our brother!"

"But how can we believe you? You are a police officer and we don't deal with the likes of you."

"I know that you don't help police officers, but you help those who are your own. Anthony was just that. When they killed him, they not only attacked me but you as well."

The growling stopped and the alley was filled with silence. The silence wasn't peaceful; no, it was the silence before a storm.

The wind blew around him. It was as if it was trying to lift him off the ground. Tyson thought that it would be safe to remove his blindfold. Slowly and cautiously he removed the piece of cloth and looked around the alley. It was empty. He removed the fold completely and sighed. Anthony's phone rang and Tyson answered it. "The shoe casing is bogus. You are gonna hit a dead end. But we'll fight with you" said the voice.

"Damn, that was cool! I need to figure out how they do it. Well, now I have an ally. Let's head out and check the cameras."

This was his big break, he had figured that these guys do not play fair and the only way to deal with them is to play by their rules.

The precinct was full of hustle and bustle, after all, this was a police station. He went to the tech area straight away. To his surprise, the area was empty except for Sam. This was a bizarre thing as this place is usually full of people. The entire place was empty!

"Hey Sam, where is everyone? I am at a loss for words, the strict tech head has finally allowed his employees some reprieve."

"Shut up Wolf! The only reason the entire lab is empty is that the captain walked in on us analyzing the footage and stopped us. He said that since this method has failed us, we should focus on something else. He asked us to make a 3D model of the alleys and find what is common."

"OK, and how does that explain anything?"

"Well, the guy looked flustered all of a sudden as if it was the most important thing. So even though it might be nothing I still wanted to be sure."

"So, did anything turn up?"

"As a matter of fact, yes. I re-analyzed the footage from all the scenes. The problem was that there is always a car that swerved in front of the person and then they disappear."

"Like it happens in the old movies then?"

"Exactly. But that is not the point. The point is that the all-knowing gang apparently made a mistake!"

"Oh wow! Do you think you could take out some time to actually tell me what it is?" Tyson drawled.

"No need to be so sarcastic. So, the point is that there is always a dent in the car, right here," he said while pointing to the fuel tank.

Opening up a comparison window Tyson slowly checked the car in all of the murders, they were all the same.

"So, Sam what do we have here then?"

“The thing is that these people probably knew the position of every single camera in the area and its angle. They knew that we would probably not look so hard, even I ignored it but as they love to taunt us they decided that they will show us a bit of that lovely plate.”

“Well, as far as I can see you can only see different parts of the plate.”

“Oh, but that’s the magic, my friend. This is like a jigsaw puzzle, albeit a difficult one. But if we play our cards right, we can at least get a partial plate and narrow our options from there on.”

“You do that, I am gonna head down to the morgue, have a cross-examination.”

“Oh yeah, I figured you would do that.”

Meanwhile, in the dark headquarters, the environment was as it was always, but it was a bit more dark and gloomy; maybe a sign of happiness now that the death of their biggest enemy had been arranged. He had to be finished off on the 14thMarch, exactly 8 days after their boss had finished off his brother. This was their most important assignment and most probably the most difficult one. Wolf wouldn’t know what hit him.

CHAPTER 8

Tyson felt humiliated because he had once again reached a dead end. Though he had the will to go on yet he had no idea on what to do. It has been two days since his brother had died, and he was nowhere close to the guy who did it. Being a detective is definitely worse than being a forensic expert, he couldn’t even cross-examine a body without permission. It was nothing a few strings couldn’t fix. Well, time to go and check the body. It was surprising though how much two bottles of vodka could help, right now he was not suicidal or murderous, but actually determined and sarcastic.

The morgue had been completely transformed. In his time as an expert, the entire wing had looked lively. Even though it only housed the dead and a man with a dead sense of humor. Now it was just… well, dead.

Today, the lab was only inhabited by Dr. King, the new forensic expert. He used to be a trainee under Tyson but due to his sudden promotion (or something along those lines), he was now the new expert. He was a middle-aged man with a large amount of grey streaks in his hair. He had dull green eyes.

"Welcome to the den, Mr. Wolf."

"Call me Tyson, I am not your superior anymore. Anyway, have the old bodies been exhumed?"

"Yeah, they just came back. It was an odd request though, I mean you checked everything in the usual mandate and a couple of extras."

"I know, but there has been a new development."

"Wait… what? What is it?"

"Till now, the detectives were looking at each murder separately and so were we…there was no reason not to, but now there is. We have discovered a clue by looking at and comparing a couple of cases."

"So, are we going to compare all the bodies?"

"Yeah, though it does make me feel glad that I asked for the bodies to be preserved till the cases were solved."

"Sorry to ask you this but do you have the permission to handle the bodies and do you want to handle your brother's?"

"Yes and No. You are going to tell me what I ask you but make sure that my brother's body is nowhere in sight," I concluded with a tone of finality, "Or the vodka may wear off," I murmured in an undertone.

"So, then let's begin by going through the stories of these victims once again."

They walked towards the autopsy tables where the exhumed bodies were very carefully laid out.

"First, we have Stephanie Hartman. Twenty-four years old, the first case of this kind to surface."

"Check the body for any sort of reaction."

"There are literally none. Look at that body, that's the body of Josh O'Reid, the only difference in these two bodies is a bruise on Josh's face and the bruise is posthumous."

"Come on! There must be something that is different. It's a gang for God's sake! It is not only one person who is committing these murders, even if it was, the chance of them being no different are as good as zero."

"True that might be the reason why there is no difference."

"What parts of the spectrum have we checked?"

"Visible, UV, and X-ray. Why?"

"Check under Infra-Red."

"But, Tyson, that's just heat signatures."

"I know that King, but the point is that these people are smart. What's to say that they haven't found some way to listen in to our conversations and that's how they have been staying ahead of us."

"Yeah, but we still would've seen it."

“But what if something else is protecting it from the other spectras?”

“Wait, yeah you are right. Lemme check.”

He then went on to check the body under infra-red. The weird thing was that both King and Tyson knew that this was a shot in the dark. There was no way that they would have done something so stupid, yet when put under the infra-red, something did pop up. Buried deep inside the heart was something warm. The body had cooled after death but that part was still radiating heat.

“Can I just say that maybe Josh had some new kind of pacemaker that we don’t know about?”King asked in a tone that was under-confidence redefined.

“Nah he has no history of heart problems. How did we miss this again?”

“Uh, maybe because we never checked for it in the first place!”

“Ok smarty, I want you to check all other bodies for similar stuff get and give it to me or Sam.”

“Aye Aye captain.”

With this parting note, Tyson walked out of the morgue and back to the main building. Standing in front of the murder board he felt stupid. Somehow every time he tried to do something, anything, the plan backfired; but each time he gambled, it worked out. It was almost as if they were taunting him. As if fate was taunting him.

A couple of new collections were added to the murder board. First of those were the shots of the plate that had been taken from the traffic cameras. The puzzle was being solved by the best technicians and analysts, that is if you could call assembling something with less than half pieces solving.

Then they had found the devices inside the bodies. It was all weird and made no sense. Unless they were taunting them. Listening in on conversations was not that big of a priority considering the fact that it had been almost impossible to find head or tail of them yet it had been their arrogance that was giving him clues, no matter how insignificant they seemed.

All that aside, the point was what was he going to do about himself. In the beginning, a bit of vodka would do the job. Now it had lost its appeal. He felt ashamed that his brother, his life had been murdered and instead of finding the one responsible, he was drinking his woes away. He then tried to bury myself in the work but that only worked for around ten minutes. So, now he was at a loss for what to do.

“Wolf, come here, quick!” Sam called out.

He stood up and started walking towards the tech center. The center was completely transformed. All around there were various snapshots of the plates, and all the computers had the specific pieces being moved around.

“Wolf, I have checked the bugs that you got me and believe me they are phenomenal!”

“They must be to get you excited like that, Sir.”

“Wolf, what happened?”

“Nothing Sir, I just wish for the geek outburst to get over,” I smiled cheekily and he grinned back.

“OK, so the bugs are just one way, but not the way that we imagined it to be. It’s a mike, Wolf.”

“A mike as in a microphone?”

“The very same!”

"But why would someone want to plant a mike in a dead body? Especially knowing that it was going end up at a police station?"

"If you think that's the odd part, listen to this," he clicked on the play button. To my enormous surprise, a very heavy voice was heard.

"We are back, stop us if you can. The falcon will reign."

What could this mean? After all, to any history geek, the falcon had been a king of Egypt. But could this have meant something else as well, why would a gang behave like a cult? Could this be more than just a simple gang?

"That's not the only thing," Sam's voice interrupted his thoughts.

"The mike can also be controlled via satellite, in fact, that is the only way, I had to install the play button."

"So, you mean to tell me that they have been telling us when they are about to murder?"

Sam gave a weak nod and Tyson felt disgusted. He couldn't help but feel guilty as it was somewhat his fault. If he had just found the damn device earlier, so many lives would have been saved.

Deciding to take a break, he walked out of the tech lab only to be startled by the same voice, yet this time it was a different message.

"Listen up, Wolf you decided to poke a sleeping lion, now deal with it. The noble falcon is out for you and you better watch out."

Looking up from the contraption, I saw Sam's pale face. He looked as if he had just seen a ghost.

"Wolf you better hurry, tonight there is going to be another murder and you need to stop it."

"But now, I have no idea where or how am I supposed to stop it."

"I don't know, usc your imagination."

Tyson walked out of the room while shaking his head. What was he supposed to do? Without realizing, he had reached the office of the Captain.

"Hello Tyson, I am so sorry to hear about your brother," he said softly.

"Hello, Cap. I need some help."

"Is it related to your case?"

"Yeah, we have a lead that leads me to believe that there is going to be another murder tonight. I just don't know where."

"How about I help you with that? You remember me denying your request?"

"Yeah."

"Well, that was because you didn't have a reason, now you do. Go talk to that guy."

"Wait, what? Just like that? No be careful or don't kill him?"

"I trust you Wolf, a couple of days ago I would have refused flat out. I would have sent someone else. You used to be too impulsive but now you've grown up."

"Jeez, thanks cap."

Tyson walked out cracking his knuckles, ready for a bout of action, after all, it isn't everyday that your mission reaches a step forward. Cap was right, he won't be taking any actions that cross the boundary.

Walking into the holding, he looked at the fearful eyes of his prey, "Time to play little buddy."

CHAPTER 9

Even as Tyson said these words, the target in question transformed. From the scared and sniveling fellow, he grew into a confident man. There was no longer a slouch, his back was straighter than anyone Tyson had ever seen. It was unbelievably stiff. He had gained a smirk, an infuriating one at that.

"Oh, it's you, welcome!"

"And pray tell, why would you sound as if you were awaiting my arrival?"

"Maybe... I was," he said with a cruel glint in his eyes.

This was a red flag. This meant something. After all, a murderer he have never met, except the one time when he had arrested him was awaiting his arrival."

"And how is your brother, if I may ask?" he said with a hint of a teasing tone.

He would usually not admit this, but at that moment Tyson saw red. He lost all control over himself.

How dare this bastard talk about his brother? He lashed out, losing all semblance of humanity in his mind. He was now an animal. A rabid dog ready to tear at its prey.

He walked three comfortable yet quick steps with the practiced ease of a boxer. Reaching him, Tyson packed in a quick barrel of punches. He continued to punch him, kick him, just use him as a punching bag. It was because of this scumbag that he lost all that was left of his family.

A punch to the ribs, "Congrats." A kick to the face, "Now I am truly alone."

That was all he could manage to say before nearly beating him to death. He lost count of the number of blows that were laid on the prisoner.

“Enough”, he said with that infernal smirk, “Are you here for information or execution?”

“Well, since you know of my true purpose, how about you help me along the way, huh?”

“Nah, I’ll pass,” he said in a cheeky tone

“When will you realize that you aren’t in control of the situation and neither is the falcon?”

“How about when I actually am not?”

“Why are you under the illusion that you are in control?”

“Because I am. From the very moment this began, though I would have appreciated the absence of the shot or the beating,” he said smiling smugly at Tyson.

This was shaping out into more of a trash-talking session rather than an interrogation.

“Well, let’s call the cavalry,” Tyson muttered.

He walked out of the holding cell and asked for someone to come in and inject the guy with a dose of Sodium Penthanol. A truth serum should be enough to give this guy what he deserved.

The patient immediately became less coherent and started mumbling things, none of which made sense.

"What is your name?" Tyson began the interrogation.

"Keith."

"Are you the member of a gang?"

"No."

"What is the falcon?"

"An Order."

"Are you a member?"

"Ycs."

"What are its motives?"

"We wish to eliminate foreign influence from the world and bring it back to its original glory, to the way it used to be in ancient Egypt."

"How many people are there with you?"

"A hundred and twenty, as far as I know."

And so went on the session of questions as Tyson continued to familiarize himself with the chain of command of the order. The surprising thing was that unlike most criminals, emphasis on most, he knew what he was doing was wrong but only did it because he thought that their motive is a noble one.

"Do you know where the next killing is going to happen?"

"Nope," he said, popping the p.

"How do I find out where it's going to happen?"

"You don't…no one ever does… until it happens, not even the one who does it."

"Is there something that can help me find it?"

"We don't strike at the same place twice."

With this clue, Tyson left the holding cell. They don't strike at the same place twice but there were still hundreds of unmurdered alleys in the city. Another troubling thing was that they weren't against a gang, they were against an entire order and this unsettled him.

He walked into the captain's chambers.

“Wolf, please tell me you found something.”

“Only thing I found was that they don’t strike at the same place twice and they aren’t a gang.”

“Shit. That isn’t much of a clue, and wait…not a gang? Then what are they?”

“They are the Order of the Falcon.”

“THE ORDER OF THE FALCON. Wolf, leave this case. The order is legendary, they always murder in a different style, and every time only one of their member is caught.”

“So, we have some information right?”

“No, the last time they were caught was at the start of World War One. We couldn’t find anything.”

“Any idea on where they will strike?”

“OH, yes. The next attack will be on the station.”

“But, he said they don’t attack the same place twice.”

“Yeah, and this building is a new one. They destroyed the old one.”

CHAPTER 10

With this, he walked out of the cabin and started to shout orders at everyone to secure the station. The station was filled with people running about, securing the prisoners. All the windows were closed, other precincts were contacted to send for back-up as it was a classified emergency. This continued for the next two hours as the entire place was secured and booby-trapped. What followed was an excruciating wait. No one dared to move a muscle, people winced at the slightest movement. Everyone was scared yet everyone was still there waiting to get the job done, no one dies tonight.

Two hours into the wait, the lift moved. Everyone was poised to strike, this wasn't supposed to happen as the lift had been shut down and all entrances were closed.

The device that we had found in the dead bodies was sitting right in the middle of the station. It would've been kind of stupid to keep such a thing in the middle of everything, what if it had been an explosive? Luckily it wasn't. They had already checked for everything possible and it had no other function, except for that voices.

"A wolf howls and whimpers," the device started to speak. It was now getting out of hand," The howl's over, now it's time to whimper."

With that, the entire building shook. This wasn't just an attack, it was supposed to be a massacre. All the lights in the station went off and all electronics stopped working. They had been hit with an EMP. This was so not looking good. Everyone held their guns as if their lives depended on it.

There was a knock on the window, everyone turned to see a guy smiling and waving at them before the window blew apart. A smoke bomb with chlorine gas flew in. The idiots were trying to turn the building into a gas chamber. Looking at the window, it was covered by a tarp. Jumping down was clearly not an option as it would hurt like hell, so they decided to go with the obvious approach.

"People, pull up your gas masks. Try to switch on your flashlights, the effect of the EMP should've worn out by now," Tyson called out.

Everyone took their gas masks out and it turned out that he was correct after all. Electronics had started to work. He sent a missed call to Danger through the fastest device he had. Anthony's phone was all the signal he needed to come out of the shadows with his team. All along they had been in the restroom as our ultimate backup.

"Everyone, Danger is here to help," Tyson called out.

"OK, so now that the pleasantries are out of the way, let's move forward. Danger," the said man nodded," Take your men and hide them in unlikely places. I want everyone to hide. The plan is to ambush them. They expect us to be near dead or already dead by now."

Everyone tried to find a place to hide when the building's lift started to work again. Turns out, the EMP had knocked it out as well and had somehow kicked them out of the mainframe, so they had to hack into it again.

The lift door opened and out strolled two people who looked as if they were made for combat. Possessing agility and grace beyond anything ever witnessed. Instead of Kevlar, they were wearing medieval armor. Something told Tyson that this wasn't standard issue, it was special. It seemed tougher, sturdier yet lighter than the ones that were usually worn at the time. Their weaponry was awe inspiring. An interesting assortment of guns, swords, and knives adorned their bodies. They calmly took out their weapons. Their masks made it impossible to tell anything about them.

Everyone was ready to shoot at a moment's notice. The eyes of their mystery assailants were darting around the room looking for people. They looked at each other and nodded. That was when all hell broke loose!

The first shot came where Tyson was hiding. He rolled out of the way to return fire. Soon they were all firing back when the tarp came off. In came three people in the same attire, ready to kill. The only difference was that they had more guns than the others. The station was heavily outclassed here.

"Bomb ho!", Tyson called out.

This was the trigger for a flash grenade, but it turned out that they were immune to that as well due to some sort of glasses that were built in their masks.

These people were hypocrites, on one hand, they talk about removing foreign influence from the world, yet they use tech like masters.

There was only one thing left to do now. That's it, it was time to get physical. There was literally nothing he could do to avoid it.

"Crass stat!"Tyson called out.

From under the tables, three of their men came out to cover him. These three were the ones who were wearing our Kevlar vests to protect them from the bullets, at least for a small duration. From behind the two assailants came Danger and his men.

Tyson came out from his hiding place and jumped at them before they could direct fire at him. He felt a burning sensation in his shoulder, signifying a shot from the window had hit him. He took one of them, the taller one down, while

Danger took the other one down. The tarp had been resealed in the window and the firing stopped.

Tyson signaled for Danger to take a couple of people and take care of what was happening downstairs.

As the men walked downstairs he walked forward and signaled for them to be relieved of their weapons. As soon as this was complete he took off their masks. The thing that surprised Tyson the most was that their armor began to beep and suddenly the armors exploded.

As he stood looking over the burnt corpses Tyson could hear similar blasts from downstairs as well, now he had a way to fight this. Their suits were explosive. This was the best option they had because nothing seemed to work on their armor.

He was going to blast these bastards to hell.

CHAPTER 11

Tyson walked around the station checking the status of his troops. They had suffered a lot of damage. Two men and some more in the surrounding buildings had killed more than half of the force. They were down to a fourth of the people in the station and half of danger's men.

Another bad news was that Danger didn't want his men in danger anymore, avenging one of their own was one thing, losing everyone to avenge that one person was stupidity.

How could this happen? They expected an attack and this is what happened. He didn't even want to think about what would've happened if they hadn't known about this.

But all that was in the past. Now they had a plan, so much of the force was lost to those idiots and all that it gave them was an idea on how to fight these people not even an idea on how to find them. This is not fair.

The only units unharmed from the attack were the tech units and the forensic unit. The only reason that they were unharmed was that they had been kicked out of the station as soon as we found out.

Tyson picked his cell phone to call King.

"King, get here ASAP."

"On my way."

They now had their forensic expert back who could analyze the bodies, even though there wasn't much left to analyze. All that was now needed was our tech expert to tell us how to deal with their explosive armor. He once again picked up my phone to dial Sam.

"Sam, I need your help… also please get your explosives kit," Tyson said with a sad smile as soon as they found out that there would be an attack..

"Huh, I don't have one Wolf...," but Tyson disconnected before allowing him to finish his statement.

He needed to find where these people were operating from and put his plan into action. There must be something they would've done to make sure that the suits would only explode due to the explosive that was fit inside and not due to any external reasons.

The next hour passed as Tyson walked around the station helping with the clean-up, checking the losses, and working out the possibilities of his plan. That was when Sam and King walked in.

Just as he opened his mouth to greet them he was cut off by Dr. King's drawl.

"Wolf, tell me right this instant what is happening? I know you are a trained medical professional but you should've let me stay. I could've helped you!"

"Glad to see you're alive as well King," Tyson said lacing his voice with sarcasm, "Now if you would be kind enough to give me permission to continue…" Seeing the two nod he continued, "So we've had losses that is correct, but the reason you were sent out is that you have no training whatsoever and would've been a liability. Also, you are both very valuable to lose. With that said, King can you help the wounded? I need to talk to Sam."

King walked out to the area where the wounded were secured. The attack had not been kind to them. They had lost their best men and this led to them being in a situation where they will have to work with not the best but what was available.

As Sam and Tyson reached the tech room which was miraculously not destroyed, he told Sam about his plan.

"Sam, the people who attacked us, they are dead. Their suites had some form of a bomb in them."

"Lemme guess: You wanna explode them."

"Yeah."

"Find some part of the explosive and I'll see what I can do."

With that done, Tyson went out to check on the ECU. As soon as he reached, a man from the ECU greeted him with a simple nod.

"Tyson," he said," we have checked the scene for the explosive device. It has been sent to the explosives department and let's just say you were right."

"What do you mean?"

"It really isn't an explosive. It's just some flashlights with a very corrosive substance. All this is controlled by a network. It is wireless but we can trace that the devices that are connected to these two."

"So, we tap into one, we tap into all?"

"Yeah."

He sent a message to Sam, to tell him what they had found.

With his job done, he decided to leave for home. While his skills were needed, he needed rest more!

CHAPTER 12

Tyson had a habit of getting in the face of the wrong kind of people, blame it upon his impulsive behavior. This time, he got in the face of a mugger taxi, and was out of bullets. The guy was smart, he had been using the standard cab where there was no possible way Tyson could reach him. Breaking the glass would mean that he give himself up and hurry up a confrontation that he wasn't prepared for.

The cabbie kept looking for his friend here and there who would help him mug Tyson. This was the usual protocol, have the rider share the cab so one person would be driving and the other could easily mug the passenger.

Tyson took his badge and kept it in front of the driver. He hit the brakes of the car and ran out. Tyson took control of the car and reached the police station. But this was not the police station, this was an old and abandoned police station. The building was at the end of the 39th street. The building had a lot of windows. It had a beautiful graffiti that signified the power of police at the front door. The graffiti read 'no one messes with us' and had a revolver painted on both sides. The text was written in pale green color and had a few blood sprinklings on it. The car had run out of fuel, so, he took the driver's phone. The screen was not working so he figured that the batteries must be dead. He had an urge to turn away and find someone, rather than entering this building. A group of young people under the effect ofalcohol were standing in front of him. He would not ask them anything because of two reasons –that he was out of bullets and they were wearing gloves and they could have a gun. They took out a gun and a water bottle. They threw the bottle towards him. They came close to him. One of them was bald. He was wearing strange clothes, a pink skirt, and a top. The other was also in a similar state. He had long hair. The person was in the dress of a gorilla. They kept on advancing and came really near him. They smelt of garlic.

The drunks forced him to drink water out of that bottle. Then, Tyson felt he could see everything, even hear and feel everything, but couldn't do anything. Whatever he was asked to do he had to do it. They dragged him to a place where a lot of people were standing in a queue, waiting for a tattoo. He was also forced to stand in the queue. A man popped out of a small door. He had almond-shaped eyes and an oval face. He was of average height and was a bit plump. He looked as if he lived in the tattoo parlor. Tyson tried to move but the man saw him.

He commanded," Get back in the line you imbecile."

He tried to ignore him but couldn't. He was a puppet now; dancing at the command of a rude man. They were divided into groups. Tyson was the leader of one of the groups called the gang. They had the task of collecting money after every crime and they were the ones who had to commit the crime.

His memory started to fade He asked one of the people around him who looked sober and was just pushed back and was told to never ask a question again.

He quietly moved back. The time of a detective was over and the new sun of a wanted criminal was rising.

CHAPTER 13

Tyson lost conscience after that. The next time he woke up, he was in a bank. It had flags of the United States of America hanging in every corner of the building. He figured out it was made up sandstone. The bank was newly constructed, and there were next to no guards. This was just a trial run for the gang.

The plump man had made everyone wear soundproof headphones and was going to give them orders from there. Before Tyson could read the name of the bank, he got the order to go inside as soon as they found out that there would be an attack.

He did as he was asked to do. There was only one guard stationed and he was taken care of. All the employees of the bank had gathered in a single room and the room was locked with a special lock that opens only from a specific signal in the ultraviolet light which will be given out by their boss when they leave the bank.

They hooked the vault to a c-4 to explode the door. This was supposed to be easy because no one else from the police department was supposed to be there but those smart people sent a scout to check if the bank was okay and the person found out that it was being robbed. He also saw Tyson helping the gang to rob the bank. They put the backup plan to work. They released smoke on the officer and ran away. This was not good, this was their first mission and would surely end badly.

That was all that happened before Tyson was gone in the darkness once again.

Tyson was alone in the small cell which had been provided to him. It very much resembled a prison cell as it also had bars. His head was spinning.

He was beginning to recall a tiny fragment of memory. It was a picture, the picture of his brother's dead body.

He remembered his mission and went to the washroom. There they wouldn't be able to force feed him the drink they made everyone else take whenever someone tried to escape.

Amidst a pounding headache Tyson tried to recollect his thoughts, his memories, his past. There were flashes. A few skills he knew. A gun that he'd stashed in his socks that they were yet to find. That was it!

Tyson took the gun and came out of the washroom and started shooting the guards who tried to stop him. He opened the bars to his cell and started running.

The first guard came towards him with a samurai sword. Tyson ducked and shot him in the knee. The guard howled in pain but stood up. Hopping towards him, he swung his blade. Tyson slid right to save him from yet another blow which was headed straight for his head. He tried to shoot the guard only to find he was once again out of bullets.

He took out a spare cartilage and inserted it in while rolling towards the left.

Seeing an opportunity to escape he sprinted towards the door. A wall of guards had started to accumulate near the door. He had to think of a backup plan. Changing his direction he ran towards the limping guard and tackled him. Lifting the guard's sword to use as a backup weapon, he ran towards the door. He shot a guard straight in his chest. Guard two had his brains splashed all over the door. Some other guards went down in a similar manner.

He then threw his gun and used his second weapon. The wall was shortening and the guards were becoming more and more scared going down easily as if telling each other, 'you go ahead, I am coming in just a second'

The last guard went down smoothly. He had his heart stuck to the sword. He was just a little kid of about eighteen. Tyson saw a band of guards scooting towards him and he simply ran out of the automatic doors. He suddenly smelt the fresh air filled with moisture which told him that he was near a beach.

A man was rushing from outside towards him.

He called," Tyson, is that really you? What happened to you man?"

He replied," is my name Tyson?"

"Man, something has happened to you. You really need a doctor, come with me."

"How can I trust you?"

"I am Michael, your colleague from the police station."

"Do you have an I.D card?"

"Of course. Come, I will show it to you."

Tyson walked towards the man. He smiled slyly; he smelt something funny was going to happen. He stopped.

He called, "Throw your I.D card towards me or I will shoot."

Tyson pretended to have a gun. The man took something out of his pocket and threw it at him. He bent to pick it up. It was a laminated card. It was a photocopy. This person was who he claimed to be, at least from the I.D CARD.

The man was of average height, not more than 5feet and 5inches. He had brown hair which covered his forehead and almost reached his eyes. His eyes were a distinctive feature. The person was a hetrochromian. One of his eyes was brown and the other one was green. He had a limp in one of his legs. Tyson felt an urge to believe him, so he did. The person embraced him as if Tyson was his brother. He pulled back from the hug.

Tyson asked, “I feel sad and angry about thinking of a brother. Did something happen to me?”

“Yes, your brother was murdered. You went out looking for the last lead and then you went missing.”

“Ok. So, did I get this final clue?”

“I don’t know. But according to me the kind of person you had become, you must have found it. Sam was rambling about it after it was announced that you had died.”

“Did I? I don’t remember anything; please take me to the doctor.”

“Yup, let’s go.”

Tyson and Michael reached the clinic of doctor Smith. A standard board with his qualifications was hung there. The door was a sliding kind. Upon seeing the green building, Tyson started to get a strange vibe. He entered and saw a tall, middle-aged, man. He jumped with surprise when he saw Tyson.

Before he could be told the symptoms, he started to examine Tyson. A couple of questions here and there and the usual.

"What has happened to you, you show the symptoms of amnesia but I guess that I should conduct a blood test."

Tyson was asked to sit on a stretcher and the doctor folded his sleeves. He tied a tube about two inches above his elbow took out two vials of blood. He went into a different room and they waited for a few minutes. The tension in the room was palpable. Then Dr. Smith came back with a weird look on his face. He cried, "What the hell? You are non-amnesic. You were fed a drug called Scopolamine."

"What is that?"

"It is a drug which influences free will. It sometimes affects your memory, if a high dose is injected. According to me, I think that I should try my specialty."

"What is that?"

"My specialty is that I can hypnotize people and I think with that I can bring back your memory."

"You think?"

"Yes."

"I don't think that we should do that."

"Why not?"

"Because you think, even you are not sure."

"I meant that I know I can do this but bringing back all your memory can be different."

"Different than what."

"Different than what I have been doing."

"So is it safe?"

"Yes, there's no harm in trying."

"If you are so confident, then let's give it a chance."

The doctor stood up and guided them to a small room. It was not too big and all the lights were out, and only a few candles were burning. He made Tyson sit in a small wooden chair. He then tied both his hands to the chair and took out a pendulum.

Just as he was about to start, Tyson said, "Why have you tied my hands?"

"Well, sometimes when you to bring back memories it brings back old wounds and it really pains so people try to run. That's what I don't want."

"Ok."

He started to swing his pendulum and spoke a few strange codes, "OlamOlah Shem."

On hearing his words, Tyson's eyelids became heavy. Hestarted to speak in English, "What is your identity? What is your truth? How did you lose your memory and what did you forget?"

Everything started to come back. Tyson had flashbacks after flashbacks. He saw a child helping another one up. Both looked like brothers. Then they grew up. One of them looked just like him and after looking at the other, he felt withering pain in his chest as if he had lost a valuable part of his life. Then he saw the dead body of the second person. He felt another jolt.

That was all that he got before he stood up. He knew what happened, he knew what he had lost. He had a well of emotions stirring in him, about to burst, about to overwhelm him. He took a couple of deep breaths, getting myself under control.

He knew what he had to do. He now had a way of getting back at those bastards.

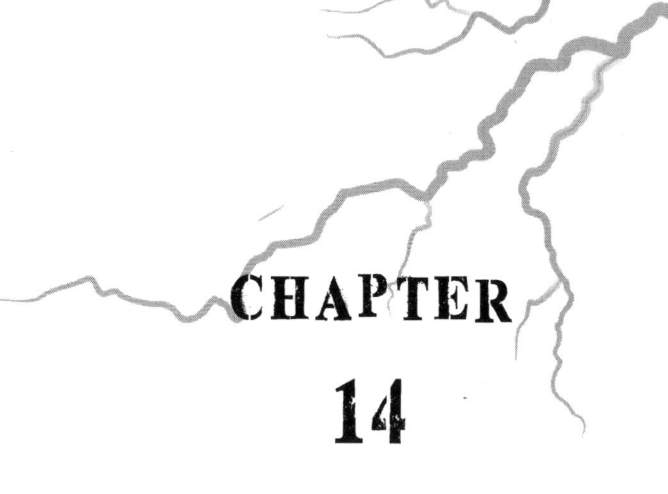

CHAPTER 14

The problem was that they couldn't find the headquarters of the order. The problem was that the guy they had caught didn't know about it, which meant that he couldn't tell them where it was, but it did not mean that he couldn't actually take them there.

The guy they'd caught had been someone who was very resistant to physical violence. Another issue was that he didn't know anything too valuable. That was what they had found out after the test with the truth serum. So, they needed some other way to coerce him into taking them there and that coercion needed to be solid, for example, something that made Tyson rob a bank.

The answer to their problem–Scopolamine.

Tyson rushed back to the police station. There was still work to be done. Sam would surely be at the station right now. He worked till late at night plus he said that he would start working to get into their system and make all the armors explode.

He would also need the help of the entire gang that Danger had because using the uniforms might compromise the mission due to the formalities.

The logistics of this mission was what was going all over his mind as he traveled to the police station. This had to be perfect, they had already lost a lot in this fiasco. Countless murders, his brother, and some of New York's finest. This had to be done with minimal casualties.

First order of business: Call Danger to see if he would be willing to come to be a part of the mission.

Second order of business: Go and check whether Sam was ready.

Third order of business: Get some Scopolamine.

Fourth order of business: Destroy the order.

Well, that was the basic outline of the plan as far as he could come up with it at the moment. Finding it prudent to start now, he decided to call Danger.

" Danger!"

"Wait, you're alive?"

"Yes, I am. Why would I not be alive?"

"Well, we have a photo of a dead body, your dead body. You were shot in the head twice. The captain issued a notice for everyone to find your body. You were announced to be dead. Tyson, to the world you have been dead for the past one month."

"One month! Why did Michael not tell me about this?"

"Tyson, you were missing for a month, God knows where. There was a guy on T.V. with your face robbing a bank. Do you seriously think anybody in their right mind would tell you about the past month before making sure that you were stable?"

"That actually does make a lot of sense."

"I know. Doctor Smith is a friend. He called me to make sure that only someone who can actually call you a friend should break this to you, who knows how it would affect your brain."

"Let's talk about that later. Were there any developments in the last month?"

"A lot of attacks and by that, I mean a lot. The device you and Sam found just gives us a warning and boom we have a new dead body. Also the recordings failed. They were a dead end."

"Did Sam say anything about the plan?"

"Yes, he did. You need to tell me about that though, only he and the cap know till now. He just goes on and on about finding the order's base so he could finally end it once and for all."

"Listen..."

With that, Tyson explained the entire plan to him. Danger was either a very good listener or, judging from all the rustling in the background, was looking for the perfect weapon to kill him. Tyson just hoped it was the first because he could not take on Danger.

"Tyson, you are either a mastermind or a lunatic. I will stand with you but I want a full pardon for all my gang members. I know it's not possible to do that for the ones already in jail, but after this, you just drop all charges."

Damn it. He should have known that Danger would not do it without a price. Yes, he considered my brother to be a member of his gang but revenge for one person wasn't enough to risk entire gang. Giving in would be unfair to a lot of people but not doing it either would be unfair to a lot as well.

"Help me do this and consider it a deal."

"I need weapons. We don't have enough for the mission."

"Lemme see what I can do."

With that, he disconnected the phone. A slight change to the plan has to be made.

New second order of business- Get some firearms. Sam was ready.

CHAPTER 15

Who knew that getting firearms in this city would be so difficult? Tyson couldn't go to the ones they usually got their weapons from and the ones who sold illegally wouldn't sell to them.

So again, they were at a dead end. As they were driving through town looking for weapons (not the smartest thing to do he knew!), Michael was on the phone with his own version of Danger. Apparently, he was not the only cop with underworld connections, a lot of cops enlist their help in exchange for small favors. This particular gang specialized in firearm smuggling, therefore the perfect place to get weapons.

"Hey, Wolf!" Michael called out.

"Yeah?"

"We got the weapons. I need you to drive to Washington Avenue. We are going to pick the delivery."

"Washington Avenue, that's a far drive. But let's go."

They went around the city trying to reach Washington Ave. Surprisingly, they didn't encounter any problems, which was a first in this case. It was a welcome change.

Deciding not to waste time, he called up Doctor King.

"Hey King, I am alive if you didn't already know. Danger has given me a run through of the past month so can we straight away get to business."

"Ty… Tyson is that… really you?" replied a very tired voice. It was as if he wasn't well.

"Yes, it is, King, in the flesh. Come on snap out of it."

"Ok…te…tell me what to do."

"I need you to call your friends at narcotics. Listen carefully King, I need you to get me ten grams of Scopolamine."

"Scopolamine!" he snapped," What the hell, Tyson? What would you do with Scopolamine?"

"Just trust me and get it, will you?"

He hated being so tight-lipped and rude to his friend. These were the people who had suffered a lot in the past month and he was not doing them any justice by behaving the way he was, but it was necessary. The lesser the number of people who knew about this, the better.

"I'll get it, he said in a dejected tone and disconnected the call.

They reached their destination a couple of minutes later.

Washington Avenue didn't look anything special. Just the usual people, the usual traffic. He wondered how they would be supplied weapons at this place. Well, until a guy literally knocked on his window asking him to open the trunk so he could put in his suitcase. Not being one to argue in such a situation, he did. The guy then placed it in the trunk and sat on the backseat. Just as

Tyson was about to turn around and get a look at his face he quickly said, "Do not turn around. I do not want you taking a look at my face. We've placed the weapons that M asked for."

That was all he said before he got out of the car and disappeared along the sidewalk. Tyson looked at Michael in disbelief as he hadn't heard him mention an order on the phone.

"Codewords," he said with a shrug.

Tyson just groaned as he revved up the engine and started to drive towards the station. In the meantime, he called Danger.

"Hey, Danger!"He said as he picked the call after a couple of rings.

"Yeah Tyson?"

"I got the weapons."

"I need inventory."

With that, Tyson passed the phone to Michael who didn't ask a question and said a couple of words that seemed like mumbo-jumbo to him. He talked on the cell for five minutes, with Tyson not understanding a single word after which he handed the cell back to Tyson with a signal to talk.

"Yeah?"

"Tyson, you have a pretty knowledgeable friend over there be sure to never lose him. On a completely unrelated note, we're in."

"Great!"

With that, Tyson disconnected the call and decided to focus on driving. He shot a couple of quizzing looks at Michael, who after ten minutes of ignoring them gave him along hard stare.

"What?"

"What code words were that? They weren't taught at the academy."

"Not everything is taught. Once you roll long enough with these people you just catch on to things."

"Okay."

After a twenty minute drive in awkward silence, they reached the station. Tyson let out a sigh of relief as the tension that had been there in the car had been killing him. They stepped out to take the elevator to the top.

As soon as the elevator doors opened and Tyson stepped out, he was attacked. Seriously, attacked. People jumped on him whooping in joy, giving him hugs. A couple of the female officers gave him pecks on the cheek that made him blush an impressive shade of red. The entire scene lasted for at least fifteen minutes with people coming back to make sure and test that he was actually alive. Finally, it was over. People pushed him towards the captain's room.

He looked as if death had warmed over. When Tyson last saw him he looked good, now he looked as if he had aged decades in the past month. He looked up, positively irritated. Let's just say that one look at Tyson made sure that he lost his breath. He froze. Slowly he smiled as he looked at him. Then with a very calm disposition, he said, "We better get Sam in here."

He picked up his phone and asked Sam to come to his cabin. Sam hadn't met him in the lobby. We waited for a couple of minutes. The tension in the room was palpable. Then Sam walked in. He was worn out and looked as if he hadn't slept for days and was running on caffeine, which he most probably was. He simply attacked Tyson when he saw him and thought it to be a fair enough punishment to just knock the air out of him. He stayed in that position for some time until the cap pointed out that if Tyson hadn't been dead a week ago, he would surely have been dead now. That made him sit down.

"So Tyson," the Captain started in a very official tone, "Tell me, where have you been the past month? Please tell me you have a way to put the plan, that Sam has been rambling about, in action."

Tyson explained all that had happened in the last one month from when he took that cab to the bank and till the very end, that is till he reached the station.

"Bloody hell! Scopolamine. Its use hasn't been in limelight since the Cora Crippen case."

"Let's just say we're desperate."

"Damn right we are. Let's call King in. He got a shipment an hour ago."

Again, they waited. Though now after two hours of explanations the tension in the room was considerably less. Now it was just excitement. A weird eagerness to just end it once and for all. While the rest of us sat with expectant looks on our faces, King walked in.

“Woah, what happened to you?”Tyson asked him cheerfully.

He shot Tyson a withering look that made him shut up. King had always been a master of the death glare. He brought out a small box that Tyson assumed held Scopolamine, kept it on the table and left. He didn’t so much as give him a look. They were supposed to be friends and he didn’t even look at him. Deciding this wasn’t the time to be down, Tyson took out his cell, called Danger and put the phone on speaker. What followed was a war council, after all, they had an Order to decimate.

CHAPTER 16

It had now been two days after the war council. All of them were strapped with their weapons. They were currently following the person Tyson had caught under the effect of Scopolamine leading them to the order's headquarters. This was the moment that all of them had been waiting for. The way to bring an end to all of this. They had a couple of police vans with them which had Danger's entire squad sitting inside and another tech van with Sam and Tyson. He would be fighting but was just finalizing the details with Sam.

"Ok, so Tyson, your job is to get as close to the center of their base, because the signals transmitter will be attached to your suit."

The basic plan was that they would go in trying to kill these people without killing a lot of them. His suit had a transmitter attached to it that will be transmitting the signals that had made the suits in the station explode. Since they didn't have a device of sufficient range to blast them from minimal contact in the field, they would need to get close and the only way to do that was to fight. He had one transmitter and Danger had the other.

There would be a ten-minute window as Sam started the signal and tuned it to the right frequency. They could've done that already but they didn't want any suits to explode by mistake and alert them of the new weapon that they had.

They reached a run down building that looked as if it would fall with a good shove. The man started walking down to the basement. They let him go. There would be a ten-minute window where they would be warned of the impending attack so they could sit up and they could kill them. They had seen the damage two suited men could do. Hundreds of unsuited with even one suited would be decisively worse for the force.

Ten minutes passed in a very tense mood. All of them waited expectantly for something to happen. They were weary and stressed. They had to get this over with and then the first guy came out. That was all the signal they needed to start fighting.

Men rushed out from both the building and the van. The fight was pretty one-sided. THE ALLIANCE WAS BEING MASSACRED.

The fight started off with a couple of flash grenades and smoke bombs as distraction. It didn't work on them. These people just smiled, pulled out masks, and started to fire again. Fire was focused at their head as that was the only unprotected part of their body while the Order had a full range of targets to fire at.

Tyson signalled his troops to move in pincer formation. Only ten minutes of distraction was required over here.

The pincer was completed in three minutes and that is when everything started to go to the dogs. The entrance was blocked. Tyson had to get into the basement to where their back up was strapped.

Tyson called for backup. There was a new wave of soldiers from Danger's squad that came out and tried to help them,. There was a call for cover. The good guys were falling… and boy were they falling fast! Tyson said a quick prayer and ran. Shooting three people in the head, he slipped into the staircase and hid in the first place he could find. Seven minutes were over, three left to go.

He caught his breath for one minutes and then slowly tried to find his way. Not even ten seconds in and he found the room where they were sitting around, looking at the T.V. analyzing their performance and forming further plans for the battle.

"Tyson, we're ready to go," Sam's voice said in his ear.

"Go!"

Tyson then sent out a flash grenade and threw it in the room. That's when all hell broke loose. BUT this time for them.

The signal had started. Tyson rushed in knowing that he could be harmed by the explosions. They started exploding one after the other. Some of them tried removing their armor but couldn't. A couple were smart and decided to attack him. Thank god for the Kevlar, and them being disoriented he just got shot in the limbs. Then all he knew was darkness.

CHAPTER 17

When he woke up, he was in a hospital. There was a doctor standing over him checking his vitals, asking him how he was doing but he couldn't say anything. His throat felt as if it had sawdust pushed through it. His eyes hurt due to all the bright lights. Everything was fuzzy and he couldn't put a finger on anything except the pain. Then it all became dark again.

This continued for the next couple of weeks. He slowly recovered under the careful eyes of the doctors. Apparently, most of the bullets had just grazed by with a couple of them actually hitting the bone. He would recover.

Weeks turned into months as his friends came to see him and give updates. They'd been lucky. The Order had been having a meeting when they attacked and all of them had been decimated.

Tyson rested, getting bored, aching to just get out of there but he was also sad. A part of him was lost. Now that the adrenaline was gone, he was finally left to face the death of his brother. He mourned for him, becoming more and more serious as the days passed. His inherent sassy behavior was slowly buried under the guilt. He had led so many men to their deaths just to avenge one. Danger died that day, so did the captain. But no one blamed him. They should. He was the one who led them, but they didn't. He knew where the blame should be put, on him and that is exactly where he will place it.

So, he healed, desperate to get back on the job and become busy. Three months later they allowed him to get out of the hospital. Another week of bed rest after which he returned to the station.

The building looked exactly the same, the people a bit wary of him but who could blame them. He just smiled and walked as if he was not bothered at all. His friends came and gave him quick hugs, trying to coddle him to death. The new captain told him that he needed to be more methodical in his job and that disorderly conduct would not be tolerated. He then smiled and told Tyson to expect an award.

He received a call and was assigned a new case. He sighed and got up. Let's get this done with, hopefully, it won't be something as high class as his last case.

THE END.

ABOUT THE AUTHOR

Harshit Bhasin is a 17 year old, born on 6th March, 2001, from New Delhi, India. A student of DPS Dwarka, he enjoys writing and reading with an equal passion. He is an avid public speaker and participates in various events on a regular basis. He has won various regional, national and international awards. He is currently appointed as the President of the school. He has a deep passion for Genetics and Astrophysics. He has also written a book previously, named 'Map to the Secret Dragon Cave'. Harshit was recently awarded the 'Student of the Year' award by NIE (Times of India).

IBD
20893
25.8.10